Nini
Here and There

Anita Lobel

Greenwillow Books
An Imprint of HarperCollins Publishers

Nini Here and There

Copyright © 2007 by Anita Lobel

All rights reserved. Manufactured in China.

www.harpercollinschildrens.com

Watercolor paints and white gouache were used to prepare the full-color art.
The text type is 24-point Neutra Text-Demi.

Library of Congress Cataloging-in-Publication Data
Nini here and there / Anita Lobel.
"Greenwillow Books."
 p. cm.
Summary: Fearing at first that her family is going on vacation without her,
Nini the cat ends up traveling with her owners to their new home.
ISBN-10: 0-06-078767-8 (trade bdg.) ISBN-13: 978-0-06-078767-7 (trade bdg.)
ISBN-10: 0-06-078768-6 (lib. bdg.) ISBN-13: 978-0-06-078768-4 (lib. bdg.)
[1. Cats—Fiction. 2. Moving, Household—Fiction.] I. Title.
PZ7.L7794Nin 2006 [E]—dc22 2005022186

First Edition 10 9 8 7 6 5 4 3 2 1

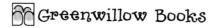 Greenwillow Books

To Nini and Billy—there and here, of course

"Oh no," Nini thought. "They are going away. They are going without me."

Nini lay down on top of a suitcase.

She stretched out on a mound of shoes.

She climbed onto a box of books.

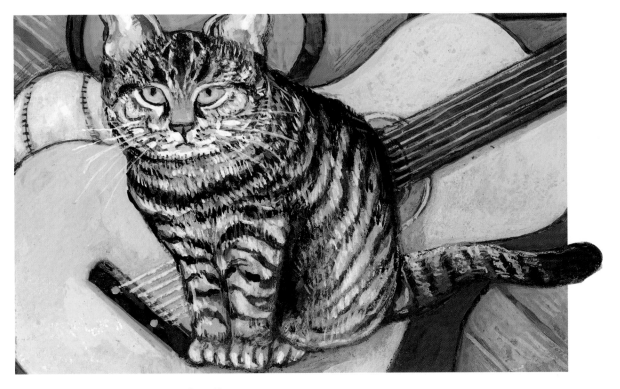

And she sat on a guitar.

Then Nini saw the big black thing.

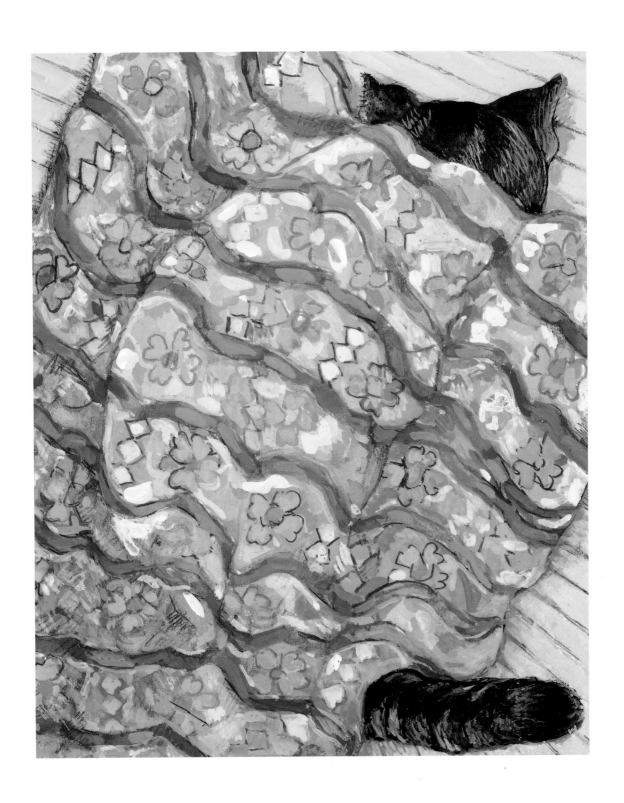

She tried to hide. . . .

No use.

Nini was caught.

"Come on, little cat. In you go."

Zzzzzzzzzzzzzzzzzzzip. . . .

Nini meowed,

and meowed,

and meowed.

Her meows got smaller...

and smaller... and smaller...

until she fell asleep.

Nini the cat was floating on a cloud . . .

flying in a hot-air balloon . . .

sailing on ocean waves.

She was bouncing on the back
of an elephant . . .

and on a rocking horse.

All at once the rocking and bouncing

and floating and flying stopped.

There was a bump. . . .

Zzzzzzzzzzzzzzzzzzzip. . . .

"Come on, Nini. Out you go, little cat."

Birds and butterflies fluttered and swooped.

A little mouse scurried past.

A white dog came by.

Nini was not sure he was a friend.

Nini smelled good things to eat.

"Come on, Nini.

Come on inside, little cat."

Later, Nini purred on a new windowsill.

She watched the sun set

and the moon rise.

That night, before Nini fell asleep, she thought,

"Yes, everything is different.

But they did not go away without me."